Flash Digest

July 2024

Edited by
Terrie Leigh Relf

*

THE STAFF OF FLASH DIGEST

EDITOR: Terrie Leigh Relf
WEBMASTER: H. David Blalock
COVER DESIGNERS: Laura Givens; Marcia A. Borell

Cover art by Paula Hammond
Cover design by Laura Givens

Vol. I, No.2   April 2024

Contents

Stories

Illustrations

THERE'S A SALE GOING ON!!!
IT'S STILL GOING ON!!!

BUY ALL THE BOOKS YOU WANT AND USE THIS 20% DISCOUNT CODE: BOOKS2024

THIS DISCOUNT CAN BE USED AS MANY TIMES AS YOU WISH, SO TAKE ADVANTAGE OF IT!

GO TO OUR SHOP AT WWW.HIRAETHSFFH.COM

NO MASKS, NO WAITING, AND WE NEVER CLOSE!

A Little Help, Please

In the world of the small indie press we fight a never-ending battle for attention to our work, as writers and in publishing. Here's an example: big publishers [you know who they are] have gobs of $$$ that they can devote to advertising and marketing. Here at Hiraeth Publishing, our advertising budget consists of the deposits for whatever soda bottles and aluminum cans we can find alongside the highways. Anti-littering laws make our task even more difficult . . . ☺

That's where YOU come in. YOU are our best promoter. YOU are the one who can tell others about us. Just send 'em to our website, tell them about our store. That's all. Just that.

Of course, we don't mind if you talk us up. We're pretty good, you know. We have some award-winning and award-nominated writers and artists, plus other voices well-deserving to be heard [not everyone wins awards, right?] but our publications are read-worthy nevertheless.

That number once again is:

www.hiraethsffh.com

Friend us on Facebook at Hiraeth Publishing
Follow us on Twitter at @HiraethPublish1

The Sisterhood of
the Blood Moon
By Terrie Leigh Relf

For thousands of Earth years, the Transgalactic Consortium has had an invested interest in this planet and its inhabitants, the Haurans. While the Sisterhood of the Blood Moon and the Guardians work together with the Consortium and Haurans to restore balance to the universe, the Blood Moon is fast approaching. The power of this moon reveals untold secrets . . . including the sacred covenant with the Mora Spiders. There is an ancient pact that continues to be honored - but at what cost and for whose purpose?

The world may come to an end. But will there be a chance for a new beginning? And if so, where?

Type: Novel – science fiction/fantasy
Cover price: $14.95
ISBN: 9781087929927

Ordering link:
Print Edition:
https://www.hiraethsffh.com/product-page/sisterhood-of-the-blood-moon-by-terrie-leigh-relf

The Saint and the Demon

By t.santitoro & Ron Sparks

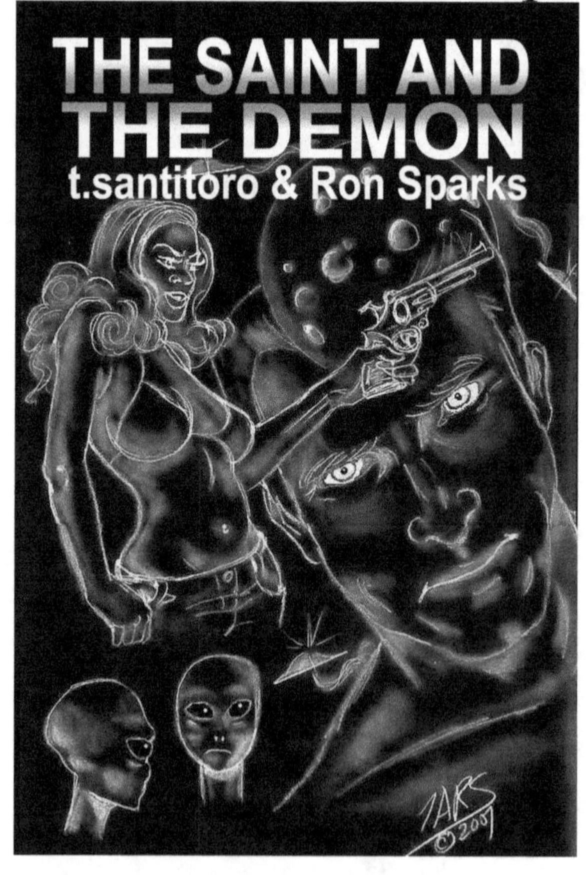

In the not-to-distant future, a young reporter reluctantly agrees to interview a senile old man in the heart of the Florida Everglades. In the humid, swampy environment, the reporter is sure that there can be no story of substance here, but the old man reveals that, in the past, his love was so strong and so passionate for a woman that he stopped at nothing to get her back when the forces of war tore them apart. He became a hero and a coward, a lover and a fighter . . . a saint and a devil. In his quest to rescue the woman he loved, he became something that she could no longer love.

Into the middle of this personal ordeal tumbles Cutter, a man from another world, sent to Earth to establish a breeding mission for his endangered race. He falls in love with an Earth woman, and must defend not only her, but also the future of his own people. The object of his alien affections, an innocent young woman named Angel, finds herself suddenly thrust into a world of aliens and intrigue, and of a love that has far more dangerous consequences than she could possibly have imagined.

Type: Novel – science fiction

Ordering Link:
Print ($13.95): https://www.hiraethsffh.com/product-page/saint-and-the-demon-by-t-santitoro-and-ron-sparks
PDF ($4.99): https://www.hiraethsffh.com/product-page/saint-the-demon-by-t-santitoro-ron-sparks
ePub ($4.99): https://www.hiraethsffh.com/product-page/saint-amp-the-demon-by-t-santitoro-amp-ron-sparks

The Gifted
By Tyree Campbell

DEDICATED TO THE MEMORY OF MELISSA MEAD

The year is 2045. Earth's societies have fallen apart for various reasons—economic, social, political, disease. To live, people began to loot, kill each other, and generally get by from day to day. In the latter stages of this deterioration, fear of disease caused immunizations to be rushed into production without proper testing. Some parents soon discovered that the children born were deformed in some way: flippers for hands and/or feet, missing organs, scales for skin, etc.

In addition to flippered hands and feet, Wendy Meade was gifted with some psi abilities that enabled her to talk with animals and with people. Now an adult woman, she scrapes by in a woods above a bay on the coast of southern Oregon, where there is an abandoned town where food is still available in convenience stores. She supplements this with shellfish from the bay. Such is her life.

Until one day she discovers that she can telepath with animals and people. A small community begins to form around her. Now, if possible, she has to use her powers to protect them from marauders.

Type: Post-Apocalyptic Novel
Ordering links:
Print: https://www.hiraethsffh.com/product-page/gifted-by-tyree-campbell
ePub: https://www.hiraethsffh.com/product-page/gifted-by-tyree-campbell-1
PDF: https://www.hiraethsffh.com/product-page/gifted-by-tyree-campbell-2

Guerrillas Just Want to Have Fun

Scott Talbot Evans

I sit all day in a metal room with no windows; the walls are plastered with computer screens. My coworkers are all robots with chrome faces, wearing dark blue military uniforms. We are a dying breed, soldiers. My friends think my job is like Rambo, but really I'm just a computer geek.

I'm the only org in this antiterrorism unit. The bots run everything, but they keep one meat sack around just for the human touch.

Their metal fingers type so fast their fingers are a blur. Their glass eyes monitor screens scrolling thousands of bits of data per second, without blinking. They are unable to feel a sense of monotony. I'm not so lucky. For me this job is dead boring. Sometimes their methodical clicks and taps drive me crazy.

We haven't seen much action since the great purge. But still, a few illegal weapons keep popping up out of the woodwork. Our unit confiscates on average about seven guns a day. At this rate, we should have them all in a thousand years.

There are always small militias and extremist groups popping up, and of course, lone psychos we have to keep an eye out for.

We're good at our job. Only fifty years ago, there were hundreds of thousands of gun deaths every year. Now, it's only several hundred in the whole world. Statistically, that is zero.

My job is monitoring online discussion forums for viable threats. The highlight of my day is when some looney tunes gets riled up and posts something inflammatory.

Looks like I got my wish. Here's some flamebaiting heating up on Politics&Religion DotHub. These are always fun. I flag the thread in question: FREE_GOSUMI_NOW.

Two users are ranting at each other. But these aren't just nacho nerds. Our team has linked these accounts to two flesh and blood organizations. Each has only about twenty members, but that's our job, to nip these in the bud before they turn into movements.

They're arguing over the naming of a small patch of land, known as Gosumi Park. It's no bigger than a city block, an uneventful plot of grass at the intersection of Main and Clinton, with four trees, a couple of benches, and the smell of car exhaust.

No matter how much peace you give people, they always find something to fight about. They can't argue over nationality of religion anymore, so they find these little naming disputes to get out their aggressive urges. And these two groups have been known to possess illegal weapons, so I monitor the discussion closely:

RebelYeller0106: You people call yourselves religious, but everything you do is for the devil!

Guerilla1776: You stole our land and now you want to lecture us on religion!

These guys are too much. What religion? What people? We're all officially humans. Didn't they get the memo?

RebelYeller0106: Dude, why don't you go home and sleep it off.

Guerilla1776: Bro, why don't you turn on the news?

What is that supposed to mean? I press the flag button. Five bots divert their attention to this situation. One robot in a major's uniform poses as a forum user to de-escalate the conversation. Another does in-depth background tracing of the participants. Another monitors the ground location for explosives, bullets, knives, or any other dangers.

It's just people and land. There is no problem until people start fighting over labels. World Council already resolved that the park would be shared equally by the two factions. Both names would appear on the plaque, side by side, with equal billing. But that wasn't good enough. Each wanted their name listed first. It was resolved by having interchangeable plaques. One would be displayed Mondays, Wednesdays, and Fridays. The other on Tuesdays, Thursdays, and Saturdays. Sundays would alternate. But still, the stupid people found the leap year to fight over, and every four years, on leap day, this little war erupts.

We have a hundred cameras recording the action in the park from every possible angle. The mob has gathered around the World Peace Statue. On one side, thirty are shouting "Free Gosumi!" An equal number on the other side are waving banners that read, "Peace or Else!" All the faces are dirty with anger and their mouths curl downward with detest.

An alarm breaks the sterile humming of the mainframes. *Ding, ding, ding.* The resonance monitor has picked up the presence of a gun somewhere in the park. We are at red alert. All the bots scramble into emergency mode.

From the audio feed of the park comes a pop. I don't believe it. Someone fired a gun.

Faster than I can see, the major to my left hits a button, and a space satellite fires a laser, instantly vaporizing the bullet into a puff of smoke which wafts gently away, just meters short of its intended target, a little girl, completely unaware of the danger.

Hundreds of police drones swarm in like angry wasps, dropping nets on everyone. The red-faced combatants scream and roll on the ground. Some struggle to break free, to grab or choke anyone or anything, but they can't. Fight over.

Such things are no longer tolerated. That's how we eliminated war, and we're certainly not going to let a few hotheads ruin it for everyone.

The police take control of the scene. All the detainees are collected and brought to a room where they are made to sit and talk out their differences. No food, no water. No one leaves till they bang out a peace deal.

***

Aliens & Others
By G. O. Clark

From out of left field, beyond the Pale, farther than stars, nearer than you think. G. O. Clark, telling stories in Bradburyesque fashion, takes you to the odd sides of life, where what you think is real might be an illusion, and what you fear might be real, is.

Ordering links:

Print: https://www.hiraethsffh.com/product-page/aliens-others-by-g-o-clark

PDF: https://www.hiraethsffh.com/product-page/aliens-others-by-g-o-clark-1

Tales From the Quantum Café
by Alan Ira Gordon

A collection of oddments created over lunch—you'll find them in this volume. There's an homage to the Thimble Theater; a treatment of the Revolutionary War in terms of a baseball game; small-town environmental problems; a random pun here and there; life on the Outback; the secret of the Drake equation; an off-beat look at Disney; and much, much more!

https://www.hiraethsffh.com/product-page/tales-from-the-quantum-cafe-by-alan-ira-gordon

Nefarious & Nightmarish
By Meagan J. Meehan

A paranoid truck driver fears aliens but learns that there are even worse things than being abducted; a wealthy bratty girl meets her match when she discovers a genie-like creature in a trunk; two hunters become the prey; a disturbed and sadistic teen learns he isn't the only monster in his community; a security guard has been pursued by the grim reaper since babyhood yet, when it finally catches up to her, she is surprised by its ultimate intentions. These and more encounter strange evils and nightmares. Read this one with all the lights on.

Type: Short story collection – horror

Ordering Link:
Print: https://www.hiraethsffh.com/product-page/nefarious-nightmarish-by-meagan-j-meehan
PDF: https://www.hiraethsffh.com/product-page/nefarious-nightmarish-by-meagan-j-meehan-1
ePub: https://www.hiraethsffh.com/product-page/nefarious-nightmarish-by-meagan-j-meehan-2

Gothic by Sandy DeLuca

Details
Pamela Love

When the newly-crowned Empress of Earth called out, "Archivist Gregory!", he stifled a yawn and shuffled toward the throne. There were dark circles beneath his eyes, yet as he rose from his bow, there was a glint of triumph in them as well.

The Empress raised an eyebrow at the old man's brown robe, as wrinkled as his face. What a contrast to the magnificent silver-buttoned uniform of the Imperial Navy's Admiral, whom she had just confirmed in his post. "Archivist Gregory, it is your turn to justify your position. Why do We need anyone in charge of the Empire's ancient records? What relevance have they to Our current rule over all of Earth's peoples?"

"Because I have discovered that not all of Earth's peoples acknowledge Your rule." Gasps echoed throughout the great hall, stopped only when the Empress raised a hand and gestured to the archivist to continue. "Mermaids have never sworn fealty to the Empire."

"Preposterous!" The Empress tossed Her golden curls, nearly dislodging Her equally golden tiara, placed there only that morning. "Everyone knows Our Ancestor, the first Emperor of Earth, conquered the world a thousand years ago, sea as well as land. Ever since then, at every coronation, a representative of each subject race must swear fealty on behalf of the others. Elves, gnomes, fairies, and all the rest have always done so. How can it be no mermaid ever has without their absence being noted?"

Gregory shook his gray head. "Nevertheless, Your Majesty, the Tower of Imperial Records lists all those in attendance at every coronation for the past millennium, including yesterday's. My apprentice and I have combed through each account." In fact, they had spent the night doing so, in a last-ditch attempt to keep themselves from being dismissed from the Imperial Service. "No one described as a mermaid appears in any of them."

The Empress drummed Her fingers on the throne's armrest. "Now that you mention it, We don't recall seeing a mermaid at Our coronation." She shook her fist. "This is outrageous! Why has no one informed the Empire of this before?"

The archivist shrugged. "Perhaps this detail has been overlooked because the Mermaids' Sea is relatively small and thus unimportant?"

"Bah! Details are *very* important." She leaned forward. "You were right to bring this one to Our attention. Your predecessors should have done so generations ago."

"Or perhaps the distance is too great and no mermaid has been able to reach the Capital in time?"

The Empress sniffed. "Ridiculous! Ice elves live at the South Pole, and they have never failed to send a delegate. She brought Us a pet penguin as a coronation gift."

"Or maybe they have never received an invitation." The archivist winced, recognizing how feeble this possible excuse sounded.

"Nonsense! Those fishtails have defied the Empire long enough. Admiral, come forth." With mainmast-straight posture, the man marched forward. "We charge you to sail to the Mermaids' Sea. Fetch one back to swear fealty. You'll have to fit out a warship with a saltwater tank first.

"If they refuse, fire a warning shot or two. The sound of cannons will remind them of their long-ago defeat. They'll soon fall into line." She folded her arms.

The admiral drew his saber. "At once, Your Majesty!"

Pointing to the archivist, the Empress said, "As for you, search out every fishtail detail in the records. Make Us a complete report. We want to know more about these mermaids."

***

Months passed, during which the archivist and his apprentice, Susannah, pored over the Tower's countless ancient texts, seeking what facts—as opposed to folklore—existed about mermaids. There was surprisingly little to be found—in fact, next to nothing.

Then one morning, Susannah, her face and hands dusty from the deepest recesses of the Tower, unrolled an ancient scroll on the table. Wordlessly, she pointed to a footnote.

The archivist read the note twice over, pulled a handful of coins from his pocket and gave them to Susannah. "Tell no one of your discovery. Go home to your village. No—wait. You're from the coast. Head inland. Find work far from the sea."

She squeezed his hand, then brushed away a tear. Her footsteps echoed down the stone steps as Gregory sat, his hands clenched before him. He dared not leave too soon. *Fortunately, I know a secret exit from the architect's drawings of the castle.*

After nightfall, he locked the Tower's door behind him. Under cover of darkness, he fled.

***

Three days later, the Imperial Guard found the archivist. *Fool that I was, to think I could ever pass for a peasant*, Gregory thought ruefully. His hands, now chained, lacked callouses. His skin was pale, compared to people who worked long hours in sun-drenched fields.

They brought him to the throne room. The Empress of the Earth crooked her finger toward the guards, and the archivist was deposited at her feet.

"Archivist, We have been waiting for many weeks to hear from you. Surely by now you must have located and read at least the official account of Our Ancestor's victorious battle over the mermaids. What did it say?"

Cringing, he said, "I took a vow only to speak the truth to Your Majesty. Therefore, I must tell you that Your Ancestor was not there, and there was no battle."

"Well, that's hardly surprising," the Empress interrupted, rolling her eyes. "Why would the Emperor bother to take command of such an insignificant military action? And of course there was no battle. No doubt the fishtails surrendered at the mere sight of one of the Imperial warships. Those pathetic creatures must have been quite intimidated and surrendered at once."

"I . . . doubt it, Your Majesty. The only reference to mermaids was a short footnote written by a ship's captain. According to him, mermaids aren't half-fish, half-human, as is commonly thought. The truth is, they're half-sea serpent—" The room darkened, and everyone turned to see an enormous mouth blocking the window, with an immense forefinger and thumb picking the teeth with the admiral's saber. "And half-giant."

Arrival at Earth-Like Planet
by Denny Marshall

Endlings
Ngo Binh Anh Khoa

The Eagle arrived at noon as it'd always done ever since the ancient days when the lofty thrones of Olympus were still occupied.

Old Prometheus, older than the whole of humanity combined, heard the flapping of its wings tearing through the hissing air, but the sound this time was odd to the god, for it lacked the usual posturing, its might subdued, its majesty dwindling in its approach.

Soon, but a few seconds later than usual, the great Eagle descended upon the bound deity, whose skin had long melted away from aeons of starvation and disuse beneath the unforgiving sun, leaving behind a giant, withered husk that had once been the mold of mankind's design.

Prometheus took in the sight of his warden as it landed. The feathers, normally graced with the radiance of divinity, had lost their golden luster, their sheen reduced to a dull and ashen remnant of their former glory, nothing more than a faded coat of armor loosely clinging to a mass of rotting skin and weakened bones.

The god stared at the Eagle, and the Eagle stared back, the prisoner and the torturer, the fated enemies and soul-bound kindred tied together in the clutch of loneliness, and now, two sentient corpses tethered to a dying world by their curse of immortality.

Out of habit, the Eagle stooped down toward the god's liver, but in a surprising move, it stopped and slowly moved back, staring at its victim with vacant eyes. And the god, long accustomed to pain, sported a barely perceptible frown in contemplation at this sudden reprieve.

"Not hungry today?" he asked his jailer.

"I'm always hungry," said the bird in a tongue only Prometheus understood, "But I don't feel like eating today." The growling of the bird's stomach subsided, but their staring game continued on, their faces alit by the red sun afar.

Prometheus said nothing, and the pregnant silence stretched on until the Eagle's voice punctured it.

"My mortal kin are dead," the bird said.

"All of them?" Prometheus asked, humming to himself.

"All of them."

"My condolences."

"Your condolences are worthless, Titan! It is your creations that killed off my kin."

"I have not offered humanity any guidance since I was imprisoned here. As such, the consequences of their actions are not mine to bear," Prometheus replied, his voice calm and steady, heedless of the bird's advance.

"You gave them a will of their own, and they think they own everything. They kill and loot, and no species or acre of land or drop of freshwater can escape their grasp. Nothing's sacred to them anymore, not the Earth, not the Gods, not even Life itself. They take and take and take, and now, everything's in ruin! Dead! Destroyed! Damned!" the Eagle shrieked, its feathers standing up in a pitiful attempt at intimidation.

Prometheus blinked. "Again, I am not to blame for the actions of mankind," the Titan spoke slowly, his soft voice carrying a unique kind of gravity as his gaze met the Eagle's in an unyielding standoff. "But I am curious. How are they doing?"

"Dying out in a barren inferno of their own making," the Eagle's piercing cry cut through the air. The Titan only hummed in response, his face a mask of indifference beneath the heat.

"What a pity," he whispered eventually, his eyes closed to combat the sudden bout of headache.

"Someone must be held accountable," the Eagle spoke after a pause. A chuckle tore through the god's chapped lips before he could rein it in.

"And who will be the judge of that? You? The gods? Please. The gods are dead, both old and new alike. I felt their existences fizzle out like storm-ravaged embers ages ago. As for the reclusive ones that did not heavily rely on belief and worship, they barely held onto their diminished souls after the total loss of faith and have long since moved on to greener pastures. Divine intervention became a lost art centuries ago. I am the last of my kind, as you are the last of yours in this expiring realm, so it would seem. Even if you blame everything my creations have committed upon my head, what will that accomplish? What punishment can you dole out that could alter the inevitable or sate your bloodlust?"

The Eagle stayed mute. It could only choke on the curses lodged in its throat and regard the Titan, the rage festering inside its being hotter than the heat of a thousand meteors. With a sudden, furious screech, the bird lunged toward Prometheus with its talons bared and beak open wide, their lethal sharpness gleaming under the harsh sunlight.

Prometheus did not flinch. He simply closed his eyes and waited for the familiar pain to come. He knew pain. He understood pain. This was familiar territory, and he would welcome it like an old friend.

But the pain did not come. The sounds of metal breaking filled his ears moments later. His eyes shot open, widening at the sight of his mangled right wrist released from its biting chain.

Before he could recover his wit, the other shackles around his left wrist and ankles were also crushed to pieces, and for the first time in forever, the Titan Prometheus was in possession of his full range of movement. With each motion, his bones and muscles groaned and cracked in protest, but within minutes, he was able to force his body to remain upright on one knee, his stature towering over the Eagle whose shadow for so long had loomed over his supine form.

"Why?" he asked, his voice a heavy rumble.

"Why not?" the bird replied, nonchalant.

"Are you not worried that I can get my revenge on you now that I'm no longer bound?" Prometheus spoke, a steely glint glowing in his eyes.

"Do as you please," the Eagle evenly stated, not bothering to move out of his enemy's sight. "You'll be doing me a service if you actually manage to end me."

Silence reigned. Prometheus stared down at the Eagle, his gaze promising violence while the creature remained still, its wings folded, unconcerned. The winds continued to hiss, and far below, the faint sounds of the ocean waves repeatedly throwing themselves against the foot of their prison rang without end, wailing as they shattered against the jagged rocks.

The Eagle's keen eyes never left the Titan, watching intently as the latter's hand reached out, his crooked and spindly fingers outstretched upon a darkened palm that opened up like an abyssal maw reaching for its prey.

But inches away from the muted feathers, the hand halted, hovering in the little space between the two before eventually retreating.

The Eagle blinked.

"Why?" it asked, a hint of curiosity sneaking past its restraint.

"Why not?" Prometheus shrugged and stretched his aching limbs. With a long, exasperated sigh, the Titan sat down beside the silent Eagle and looked at what was left of the sun in the distance. "Everyone else is either dying, dead, or done with this world. As far as I can tell, only you and I are left here, rendered powerless and forced to live on with nothing to live for. If I'm somehow able to kill you, my days will become very quiet. As grating as your voice is, it does provide me with some measure of entertainment."

The Eagle made a noise that could either be interpreted as a scoff or a laugh, but it offered no retort as it followed the Titan's gaze toward the horizon, still bleeding, still scorching, still sinking deeper into the writhing, foaming waves.

Time crawled onward until some wet and squelching noises banished the uneasy stillness, drawing the bird's attention back to its former prisoner, only to see an open palm held out right next to its face, on which a liver, freshly gouged out and still drenched in blood, laid. The god's wrinkled visage displayed no visible sign of pain.

"Want some snacks?" Prometheus asked, and the lonely peak at once became alive with the Eagle's sharp laughter soaring above the wretched howls of the winds and wails of the waves as the shroud of darkness gradually enveloped the irreparably shattered world.

The War World
Daniel Crow

Imagine the boring abundance of temporal and probabilistic flows condensed into a deliciously tight and refreshingly linear existence. Now, fill that all with emotion, rage and fury — and you get the one-of-a-kind War World adventure.

Let yourself loose on a planet where primitive carbon-based lifeforms clash in a daily — and deadly — fight for a spot under the sun.

Lounge on our comfortable orbital warp station, unseen to the planet's inhabitants, and have your mind and will be projected into the linear four-dimensional reality as a ghostly puppeteer within one of War World's now eight billion inhabitants.

From ruthless deserts to cold, snowy tundra, take a blood harvest in a variety of conflicts carefully crafted by our Experience Designers through surgically-precise meddling in the localised course of history and causality loops.

Live out the hardships of a common foot soldier or upgrade to Tesseract-tier and experience the action as an officer, war chief, or another localised dignitary.

For those willing to take it all, seize one of the limited Polytope packages and help us shape the grand narrative of the War World as one of the national leaders, kingmakers, or unseen rulers.

A warrior, a commander, a leader — condense your multifold existence into being the one in a someone and experience the exciting paradox of having everything to lose . . . And even more to win.

Are you up to the fight? Book your package today and find out.

AbracaDrabble
By Tyree Campbell

A drabble is a story containing exactly 100 words. This volume contains drabbles with various science fiction and fantasy themes. In here you'll find trolls, time travel and outer space construction problems, courtesans who take instructions literally, dietary supplements, skip tracers, and demented nursery rhymes, and much more. Some are funny, some poignant, some serious, and some are all three.

Print: https://www.hiraethsffh.com/product-page/abracadrabble-by-tyree-campbell

PDF: https://www.hiraethsffh.com/product-page/abracadrabble-by-tyree-campbell-1

They Will Come Soon
Maximiliano Guzmán

The moon in eternal agony is darkening in my eyes.

And my night is a shadow of famished monsters that refuse to devour me.

Margarita recites the Lord's Prayer.

—Don't try for reconciliations.

— I tell her pessimistically. And drying her tears, she replies: —We will be the next hosts of the party.

—But I don't see that we have prepared any party — I tell her downcast.

—Don't you see that we are becoming invisible? — she asks me, crossing herself.

—I can't see it. She, sitting next to me, brings her left hand and places it on my chest.

—When you no longer hear me nor me . . . As she says these words, Margarita takes her hand away and hesitates whether to continue speaking.

—What are we waiting for? — I ask her, watching as her face begins to disappear.

—We are waiting for them to come . . .

—Who are they? — I would like to understand her. Margarita stands up.

—I must clean, tidy up the whole house, show them that we were happy.

—Were we happy? — I ask her, forgetting the best memories. Margarita turns her head, looking at the mirror.

—They will come soon, she warns me. And I see her going from one place to another, arranging drawers, hand washing clothes, dusting the furniture, running the curtains.

She points at the Windows.

—No . . .

But I have to do it — she tells me with a choked voice.

—Why?

—When the guests arrive, we don't want to drive them away.

—But it's cold.

—Do you still feel it?

—And the crows?

— I ask worried.

—The guests will come before them, I promise you.

—Why do you think they will?

—Because they will miss us. They will want— but she stops. — It's better that we sleep.

And approaching the bed, she lies down next to me, hugging me. They knock on the door, once, twice. They just have to turn the doorknob, I think. And with a kick, the door violently falls. A policeman walks in covering his nose, followed by three firefighters who repeat the gesture. The building manager starts to cry. The neighbor from 5th C explains something about my children to the policeman. The policeman scribbles in his notebook and asks everyone present to leave the apartment. And Margarita told me they would come. I should have let her open the windows, I think.

And the firefighters return with the policeman, accompanied by other people. These new people look at us with pain and resignation. They talk about how to move us and take us to a more comfortable place, where Mariano and Clementina will recognize us.

—I thought the party was going to be here — I tell Margarita who, distressed, knows she was wrong.

—We'll be okay, we'll be okay, she replies, looking at me for the last time.

—Don't go — I tell her.

—Come with me —she tells me and I cling to her spirit, floating lightly

Between Bites by Debby Feo

A life-long lived is the dream for most of the inhabitants of Earth, but how long is too long? Come along on a journey of stars and moons, summers and winters, and all that lies in between and beyond. Learn the secrets of the vampires and see the world through their - more often than not – heart-broken, sad, and thoughtful eyes.

https://www.hiraethsffh.com/product-page/between-bites-by-debby-feo

In Dreams
Jay Sturner

Having drifted through the portal of a dead oak and grown tired, a fairy has fallen asleep in the ear of a napping man. Soon, their dreams intermingle. Such accidents can happen when realms run parallel to one another.

The young man, in his garden hammock, has lost all sense of time and earthly knowings. Purple and copper-colored hills, groves of mossy trees, sentient orchids, all imprint softly upon his psyche like the scales of a moth wing. Curious beings peek from ferns, rise out of nearby waterfalls, slink-hop along flowered boughs.... Presently his heart beats with the joy of childhood.

The fairy, cuddled along the curve of the man's earlobe, timidly ventures forth through a dreamed experience of bustling city life: skyscrapers, trains, car horns; street musicians; various aromas spilling out of restaurants. In the noise of it all she becomes lost, overwhelmed, has the odd sensation of being pinned inside something akin to a massive insect collection—a million bodies struggling to set themselves free. And yet there's something enticing about it all, electric, and it courts her heart.

In time, the two awaken from their respective naps, each returning to who they were and where they came from. In subsequent months, the man is reborn into a mystic who writes books and conducts seminars, changing many lives. The fairy—now a wanderer—veers off into the gray periphery of her homeland, her once-luminous flesh dropping off in pallid strips.

But this is not a death. For as the city-seed cracks open within, veins of a somewhat different light sprawl forth from her center; and her being pivots under its influence. A longing for jazz sets in. For city parks, architecture. Sports complexes. Libraries! And most of all, a longing to be absorbed within the spectra of human emotion—to *be* human.

Eventually her body collapses and breaks apart like a scattering of fireflies; the essence of her former self carried off on an inter-dimensional wind. One perspective shifts out for another; she enters a loving womb. Soon she'll be reborn, not in her homeland—though *of* it—but in the earthly realm, the big city. A new path along which she'll one day envision purple and copper-colored hills. Perhaps on a quiet afternoon, in a dream.

Heir Apparent
Tyree Campbell

Answering a distress call, March and Myrrha find a young woman who has deliberately been marooned on an uninhabited world. She claims to be Hoya Palologa, heir to the Palologa throne on Wanderby. But there is already a Hoya who has been invested as the heir apparent to that throne. Myrrha believes the claim of the Hoya she and March have encountered. Thus begins a journey to establish the succession, a journey made far more perilous because Hoya not only claims the throne, but is also a sinister personage with several crimes on her resume.

March and Myrrha find themselves embroiled in internal politics on Wanderby, where the slightest wrong move can get them killed. The rulers on that world are oblivious to the subtle machinations of their underlings, one of whom has created a lookalike but false Hoya. Which one is which? And will death take the real one before March and Myrrha can stop it?

Type: Novel – science fiction

Ordering Links:
Print: https://www.hiraethsffh.com/product-page/heir-apparent-by-tyree-campbell
PDF: https://www.hiraethsffh.com/product-page/heir-apparent-by-tyree-campbell-2
ePub: https://www.hiraethsffh.com/product-page/heir-apparent-by-tyree-campbell-1

Who?

Daniel Crow is a journalist and public relations professional currently based in Germany. Having grown up on Tolkien and Stephen King, he has long been in love with writing, drawing inspiration from myths and folk tales of the past. His other passions include high-tech, history, and old comedy movies.

Scott Talbot Evans won second place in *The New Yorker* caption contest, and runner-up in *The Saturday Evening Post* Limerick Contest. His short stories appear in *Amazing Stories, Shoreline of Infinity, Creepypod,* and *Crimeucopia.* He is working on his fifth book, *Pennybottom's Academy for Wayward Dogs.* For more info, please visit: https://scotttalbotevans.wixsite.com/scott-talbot-evans

Maximiliano Guzmán was born in Recreo, Catamarca, Argentina. He studied Film and Television at the National University of Córdoba,

Argentina. He is the author of *Hamacas* (Zona Borde Publishing), an editor at the digital magazine *La Tuerca Andante* (Argentina), He participated in the International Anthology Sucio de Letras from *La Tuerca Andante* and the *Anthology of Hard and Erotic Science Fiction* from Editorial Solaris of Uruguay.

Ngo Binh Anh Khoa is a teacher of English in Ho Chi Minh City, Vietnam. In his free time, he enjoys reading fiction and writing speculative works, many of which have appeared in *Star*Line, Weirdbook, Spectral Realms*, and other venues and anthologies. He also enjoys writing haiku, some of which have won awards and achieved honorable mentions in international contests in the US, Japan, Canada, and elsewhere.

Pamela Love was born in New Jersey. After graduating from Bucknell University and working as a teacher and in marketing, she turned to writing. Her speculative fiction has appeared in the anthologies *Havok Season Eight: Vice & Virtue, Wyrms: An Anthology of Dragon Drabbles*, along with *Luna Station Quarterly* and *Tales From the Moonlit Path*, among other publications. Her work is also scheduled to appear in the upcoming anthologies *A Little Fantasy Everywhere* and *Dragon's Hoard 3*. She now lives in Maryland.

Neo-Mecha Mayhem
By Priya Sridhar

Neo-Mecca Mayhem is a cyberpunk dystopia adventure inspired by film director Satoshi Kon.

When a serial killer murders his own daughter, Corsair Heir Neil is determined to find the girl's twin sister before she suffers the same fate. To do so, he must enter Neo-Mecca, an American military base disguised as a Japanese city of the future, and warn teenage Kaori before her father kills her. He finds himself unable to tell Kaori, however, wracked with guilt and trauma. Kaori, kind and oblivious, refuses to believe she's in danger. Corsairs steal possessions and people to protect them from harm, but Neil is new to the Heir job with his elder brother murdered in the line of duty. He doesn't want to steal anyone. Things only get worse, however, when Neil's sister Nia barges in, determined to keep Neil safe by any means possible and to keep Kaori in the dark. The future has never looked more glittery, or deadly.

https://www.hiraethsffh.com/product-page/neo-mecha-mayhem-by-priya-sridhar

www.ingramcontent.com/pod-product-compliance
Lightning Source LLC
Chambersburg PA
CBHW070613160726
48003CB00005B/2257